# QUARRY

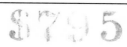

UNIVERSITY OF UTAH PRESS POETRY SERIES

CAROLE OLES

# QUARRY

UNIVERSITY OF UTAH PRESS    SALT LAKE CITY    1983

University of Utah Press Poetry Series
Dave Smith, *Editor*

Published by the University of Utah Press
Salt Lake City, Utah 84112
ISBN 0-87480-217-2
Printed in the United States of America

See Acknowledgments, page 81, for permission statements.
The author wishes to thank the National Endowment for
the Arts and The MacDowell Colony for aid and encouragement.

The paper in this book meets the standards for
permanence and durability established by the
Committee on Production Guidelines for Book Longevity
of the Council on Library Resources.

Library of Congress Cataloguing in Publication Data

Oles, Carole.
    Quarry.
    (University of Utah Press poetry series)
    I. Title.
PS3565.L43Q3    1983    811'.54    83-1158
ISBN 0-87480-217-2

*for my mother*
*and in memory of my father*

"Therefore, when we build, let us think that we build forever. Let it not be for present delight, nor for present use alone; let it be such work as our descendants will thank us for, and let us think, as we lay stone on stone, that a time is to come when those stones will be held sacred because our hands have touched them, and that men will say as they look upon the labor and wrought substance of them, 'See! this our fathers did for us'."

— John Ruskin

*The Seven Lamps of Architecture,*
"The Lamp of Memory"

"What a marvel to be wise,
To love never in this manner!
To be quiet in the fern
Like a thing gone dead and still,
Listening to the prisoned cricket
Shake its terrible, dissembling
Music in the granite hill."

— Louise Bogan

*The Blue Estuaries,*
"Men Loved Wholly Beyond Wisdom"

# FLYING OVER THE KINGDOM

Not to strafe your house
or match arsenals
but to find you

under the royal garments,
the invulnerable reds:

a serf sleeping on hay
in his sputum —

banish me if I lie.

I can still make out the faces.
I'm over the target now.

# CONTENTS

I

# STONECARVER

## for Father

Don't look at his hands now.
Stiff and swollen, small finger
curled in like a hermit:
needing someone to open the ketchup,
an hour to shave.
That hand held the mallet,
made the marble say
*Cicero*, *Juno*, and *laurel*.

Don't think of his eyes
behind thick lenses squinting
at headlines, his breath
drowning in stonedust and Camels,
his sparrow legs.

Think of the one who slid
3 floors down scaffolding ropes
every lunchtime,
who stood up to Donnelly the foreman
for more time to take care.

Keep him the man in the photo,
straight-backed on the park bench
in Washington, holding hands
with your mother.
Keep his hands holding
calipers, patterns, and pointer,
bringing the mallet down
fair on the chisel,
your father's hands sweeping off dust.

## STONECARVER'S WIFE

She waited while he drank his loss away,
now makes him drink his medicine,
won't let him stay alone.

*It could be me*, she says,
his saint, his caryatid.
She grows gardenias
in a window box
two floors above the garbage.

She is the Minnesota farm,
the miles she walked to school,
black bread she baked each morning;
her rheumatic fever
and the lasting murmur in her heart.

Her yearning in the charcoal portrait
abandoned by the stonecarver
when it smudged,
and her sorrow
at the son erased entirely.

She is her body
from which much has been taken,
what can be seen
as it houses what cannot.
The ear
into which, at 5, she slipped a caterpillar,
and the legs
that took her to the top of the windmill.

From there she could see the world
as far as it went, counties away.
They sent a man up to rescue her.

# CROSS-EXAMINATION OF FATHER

Which tree shaded your face when you asked her,
how long was she silent, what did you do with your hands?

What were you thinking inside the dark hall, climbing
stairs to the room where she waited that first July

in air tacky as fresh-varnished wood?  How did you say
the right words while the fan hummed *summer* over and over,

did you think it would never end?

Did she matter more than Lou Gehrig's name scrawled
on the baseball, what games did you privately want to win?

If you'd imagined the umpire's call, extra innings,
would you have hurled the bat, stormed off the field?

Carving doors to the Supreme Court, did you believe justice
would open for you?  Did you know, making Juno's wild hair,

that you too would be out in high winds?

Did everything happen like weather you could only dress for
not stay out of, and drink to keep warm or cool

while your heart ran ahead of you hunting the chance to believe
and came home hangdog, tired, starved?

What of me in the middle, why do I want to dive into your life
past my face on its skin?  So help you God,

is it your story, or mine?

# STONECARVER, RESTORING

### Soldiers and Sailors Monument, 1960

He kneels on top of Manhattan
turning his chisel in the eye
so the eagle can see again.

One hundred fifteen feet up, man
and bird are a single gray
animal, perched on Manhattan

where nothing reaches but rain
and the city's breath. Vandals can't fly.
When the eagle sees again

it will watch George Washington
thrown piecemeal from a horse. 'Today,
while he's kneeling here, a Manhattan

kid with a dealer downtown
is selling Columbus's arm for a high. .
But this eagle will see again.

The stonecarver remembers his Latin —
*Nil Desperandum* — and why
he kneels on top of Manhattan
so the eagle can see again.

# NOW, WHILE WE HAVE THE BODY BEFORE US

If the subject should open one eye
while we are deep in procedure,
we want to apologize.

All roads have led to this place.
The carpet must be synthetic,
the screen must get the largest
life in the room.

Let us not disregard the food —
what has been eaten, what remains —
the shoehorn to begin each day,
and the worn spot where for years
someone has stood still.

How hard the subject was slapped,
How often caught smoking,
Who sat where in the big house,
Who held the mother's hand:

all these we exclude
though we smell their presence here
like onions, long after.

We are part of this exhibit.
Look! the subject rises, bows
and offers us his place.
We argue. It's impossible . . .

But now *we* are lying down
and he is about to speak,
perhaps to say
what left through the open window.

# STONECARVER, AT WORK ON BUST OF CAESAR, THINKS OF HIS PA

## 1935

*in his shiny vest, counting the Ansonia's chimes*
*biting his cheek as I ease the lock*

*spitting* Silliness *when Ma does us the jig*
*dishtowel flying at her waist, hair unpinned*

*making me leave the presses*
*signing me on at the quarry to help*
*send his favorite to college*

*big boss of the stones!*
*the men whisper as he walks*

*at the front gate, saying before God*
*that his daughters are out, forbidding them*
*no man good enough but him*

*one grows fat*
*one smokes in her room behind the chiffonier*

*when I speak up, telling me since I married*
*I'm out of the family*
*the wife right there*

*some things you'd be wrong to forget*
*(This lip's too full.)   a warm Friday*

*fishcakes for supper, voices moaning*
*from the synagogue next door*

*the prize magnolia in bloom, and all of us —*
*Ma turning to him,* Smile, Mr. S! Smile.

[8]

## STONECARVER DISAPPEARS INTO TV

Don't kiss me, he says.
One of us is contagious.

I'm the daughter leaving, a routine
we take like vitamins.

I have something to say
but he's rejoined Todd and Valerie

and the plumber who's strumming a yuke.
They can't see him back.

Young, he drank till the world got well.
Now the screen makes him smile,

he can sit still and run.
What I want from him is infection.

## READING FATHER

The postcard you didn't send
has never doubted
its true destination: me.
It hid in cigar boxes, rode trains,
marked time four decades
in the backward countries of closets.

You never mailed it to your brother,
signed your full name.
Even distance
couldn't bring you two together.
He the baby, the darling, the only
son your father sent to Yale.

I see you at a kitchen table, taking care
as you wrote. It wouldn't do,
and you misspelled *believe*.

Was there something of home
in the postcard painting
"U.S. Capitol at night,
illumination by electricity"?

a familiar something in the empty street,
bushes dark and secret,
the bloated moon against sulphuric clouds,
the doors all closed?

The future was a town with six good bars
when you wrote the message
"I am getting settled.
I beleive I will like Washington
better than last time."

Father, hope rang once
in your pockets.
Since then, too many last times.

# LIKE MUSICAL CHAIRS

My father sits at my right hand
at the dinner table. I try to ignore
him clawing his way breath to breath
hanging from the edge of his life.
This is his power, to take us with him
in a hail of rubble and roots:

my son, dropping his fork,
his eyes
searching my face for safety
against someone too big

my daughter, swallowing hard
a mouthful of dough
as her brow assumes
the downswoop of sorrow.

Whoever my father once was — joker,
brawler, stonecarver, firebrand, lover —
is consumed by his body,
is the weight he has lost.

I want to tug at his sleeve, interrupt
*Look, I'm here too!*
But he makes his way between minutes
in a game of musical chairs,
expecting silence mid-measure
and himself to fall, chairless,
through the floor of the world.

# FOR FATHER, AT 112 POUNDS

Astronaut of the livingroom,
how far can you venture
on the umbilicus that hooks you
to your oxygen supply?

In perennial pajamas
that billow, clown
around your stalks of arm and leg

you are so much structure
refusing to fall down.
Jaws, forehead, base of skull,
backbones like vestigial wings:

my daredevil, you confound,
enthrall. How small can you become
and still not disappear?

King of the realm
of my childhood, benevolent despot
who taught me to play fair

now you whisper
*Why don't they give me a needle
and stop this.*

O Father, let
me touch the crater of your cheek,
fill the black holes
at the center of your eyes.

## BACK, SAYS THE VOICE

*Back, says the voice from the groin.*
*Back under your first pillow*
*below the mother's ribs,*
*between the gasp and the sigh.*
*Stay. You will be fed later.*
*But not in this house.*

*

The game: going limp at the curb
the child is lifted between them,
swung out into space,
she their center,
their touch wired
through her.
*More!* at the other side,
the next crossing, and next.
They tire.

*

Out walking, the three of them,
Mother in her big dress,
*Rabbits*, the boys on the corner giggle.
*Why*, the child wants to know
looking up at her, then him,
squinting against the light
behind their heads.
They look at each other.
*Nothing*, they say.
She knows they mean everything
and runs
until they shout *Wait*.

*

*Sheet thrown off,*
*they curl close.*
*The child is up first, thinking*
Shh. He's asleep.
Look at that beanbag.
*Wanting to rattle it.*

\*

She's always there.
He leaves, and comes back.

She brings oatmeal and the smell of starch.
He takes the child ice-skating,
teaches *glide, glide,*
*fall like this.*

Her hand is cold milk
on the burning forehead;
his a shell
into which the small hand can slip.

She a lake, and the shore around it.
He the gale that comes without warning,
the trees it breaks.

She sews the scraps into usable garments.
His photo, Stonecarver at Work,
appears in the *Herald Tribune.*

\*

*Years over the wall, a man waits.*
*Take a cloak from the house*
*for your journey.*
*Whose will you wear?*

\*

Christmas Eve day:
the father late,
air ready to crack
at the sound of his key.

Six false starts
and the door flies open.
He pirouettes in,
a slow-motion film of himself
walking a tightrope.

The mother is braced for his voice.
It comes like an earthquake
clattering cups on their hooks,
a sick-sweet afterwind.

She forgives him again, cries
into her arm on the table.
Becomes the road for his travels,
the water for his thirst.

What is her shape by moonlight,
when no one is calling?

The child must have done something wrong.
She learns to kneel like her mother.
Meanwhile, in the back room of her head
a rebel is plotting
the uprising of knees.
She sharpens herself at the grindstone,
she sparks.
They leap out of range.

*

*None return without leaving.*
*Climb to the man who waits.*
*Wave goodbye.*

*

Your name for his,
Father.  It's legal, right
that we lie here together,
a perfect jigsaw
of notches and bulges.
Twice I have swallowed
his magic fish,
hiccuped it back into air
wearing ears
and somebody's nose.
Stay out of it, Father
on the other side of the wall,
your stale cigar smoke
a spy at the keyhole.
I'm not 15 and surprised
in the back seat of a Chevy.
I'm not kicking too high
or bending too low.
I've only learned
what you never would tell,
you with the babe on your keyring,
you with the glossy nudes
in your handkerchief drawer.
You go to sleep now.
Stop listening.  It's over
between us.  I go home with him.

                    *

              *Later come back*
              *through a gate in the wall.*
              *This is that gate.*

                         *

Later:
       after the deaths of uncles and aunts,
after the child has a son like the one
they lost, and stops clenching her fist
to hide the long lifeline.
After their train and hers leave for separate cities,
baggage stored overhead.

When she turns to find them, amazingly, with her
— all three leaning into the same curve.

*

The father looked as if he'd walked far
in a duststorm:
the fine white on his hair,
stuck in his eyebrows,
mapping his frown,
growing out of his nostrils,
in his pockets, cuffs,
his footprints.

He'd been with stone

> *Name the hand*
> *that carves statesmen and gods*
> *to stand in the weather.*

Henry Reginald Simmons,
Reggie, "Red"

he'd made them breathe
and wore the color
of their breath.

*

Art reconciles, *nil desperandum.*
Marble and words.

Let the child walk with the father
and speak of things undone.

Put the mother beside him,
her hand in his. No one between.

> *Let the book fall open*
> *and stone lips part.*

[17]

II

## DOMESTICA

Coatless, you're dropping the garbage
into the guaranteed-not-to-crack
cracked plastic barrel,
you're tasting the mouthwash of February
when the night stops you
like a sailor asking for a match

and before turning back to the light,
the warm kitchen, you look up just
a second and the stars are still
there, more reliable than love
and other electric, still polished,
still taking care of themselves.

## MICE

They leave crumbs of themselves,
a trail like caraway seeds
to say *we called while you were out.*

They walk the ledges of bookshelves
and eat our words,
they skim the pages of night.

Our house tells them the secrets
behind walls, under floors,
where flashlights can't shine.

Once I saw one blunder out, whisk
along the tiles into nowhere
before I could decide what to call him

though I knew he was someone
I'd cross the street to avoid —
that gray dart, that non grata machine.

Something has to be done.
I re-run debates between good
and evil. I think of multiplication,

disease, war, and space-sharing.
I think of my own neck.
Won't it take more than a nest of

spared mice to make us human?
I'll set the traps if you'll chuck
the bent bodies. For we, love,

are partners, murdering whatever
small things scale our walls.

# THE CARDINAL CAUSES ME TO SAY *OH*

and stand still
(such color frightens easily)
stand, while all of winter falls away.

Against the pavement-gray weather
he wakes the shriveled lilac bush,
he rules the scrag.

The bird regards me
from above his black mustache.
Looked at, I move — he flies,

his red lifts in my mind
toward someone and the distance
that I could call winter

the ground where nothing grows
people slip and break
never see their families again . . .

Does he still wear a mustache
and did I move too catlike?  Oh
such color

shakes the barest, dunnest branch.

## SHORE-WALKING

I am wearing gray, blending
between a frame house and water.
This is only partly a nature walk.

It's a way out of the room
in which you insisted
and I left
through the cracks you spoke.

Houses shrink
as they march toward the Point,
the bellbuoys are lonelyhearts.
I take their salt message
into my skin.

I am eelgrass following the current
that pares matters down.
This gull, all bone and sockets,
smells less dead
than the place between houses and water

or musty words in beach cabins
where windows go black when the lights come on
— or the bedrooms between you and me.

I stick feathers in my hair.
The farther I walk, the more I belong.
This is not a nature poem
although I want to say,
like a beginner at English,

*The sun is shining.*
*I picked these rosehips.*
*There's poison ivy on the path.*

# CONDITIONAL

If we spent the next few years
dancing, so close that fear
couldn't cut in or call for a foxtrot,
I'd stop grinding my teeth at night
and the soft parts wouldn't recede.
You'd open the door to yourself, there'd
be a guitar, a light on inside.
We'd be facing.  Words would be outlawed
because bodies enunciate clearer
the one thing we want to hear.
For all their largesse, the trees
only say *trees*.
If we could move together in time
— not the leap over the rim,
the freefall — but dancing now,
I wouldn't care who asked who.

## SPRING

It begins with her fixation
on the endodontist
whom she admires for his artful
sublimation of the act of love.
He gets rich
when a woman opens wide
and he does what's good for her,
rubs out necrotic tissue.
Two immortal themes converge
in her, pink and quivering.
Such digging, such exposure

yet no pain. He gives forgetfulness.
They love under lights, his eyes
seeing all while hers close.
They love to music canned and faithful,
the timing always right.
No disappointments, one-night stands.
Three times until she's vivid.
All promises are kept.
He has her on film,
she has him in her mouth.

Outside, the season bites down.

# THUS, AT NIGHT, THE HEAD ENACTS THE HEART

First I lose the dentist, then my car,
then you — an incremental repetition.
I climb each hill in town and watch the bright
flotilla in the bay: the red umbrella
race. I fall in sand, swim freestyle through
the sewerpipe. Onstage, they aim the cannon
at me, shoot the excrement. The crowd
goes wild. Encouraged by success, I rise
onto the roof of the resort hotel, prepare
to leap. (My last resort.) Some grappling hook
of instinct pulls me back, the St. Bernard
is barking at my heels.
I never find you in that town I call Regret.
By day, I don't remember who you are.

# WHAT SHALL WE NAME THE SNOW?

Since it redeems the world,
how about John,
"God's gracious gift"?

Not tonight, when the storm pins us
hours apart, under
the wreckage of our houses.

Better Theodoric: "ruler of the people";
better Caleb: "dog."

If I were a child I'd name the snow
Susanna the lily, Esther the star
and lay me down in fields, constellations
to make angels.

But tonight call the snow Gertrude,
"spear-maiden"
or Mallory, "ill-omened."

Nominations like these keep my mind
from impassable roadways, lines down.
They avert the tragedy
where I collide with you

in a library of snow,
vast blank pages of indifference.

# DRIVING TO WORCESTER IN SNOW

Illumination is what's falling
everywhere. Trees lose their heads in it,
the distance comes near.
I'm trying to see
what the light is concealing.
Somebody, turn on the dark.

This isn't safe, so it's beautiful,
the way lightning crazes the sky-bowl
or wildflowers grow over minefields. The way
you stand close and then leave.

Mist shines through my skin so gently
I can hardly believe in concrete abutments.
Like in the old days when I was immortal.
Since then I've died a few times:
once by air, once by water,
and once more by love.

The world's a still place. What hits
my windshield hits softly.
Across the divider, small lamps
bring me something to read by.
I lean into the arms of the weather,
make the road as I go.

# DRY ICE

At dusk when the Good Humor man
part doctor–part cop
rang the bell on his bicycle wagon
down from our fire escapes
we came, we came like gnats
for sundaes, toasted almond, coconut pops.

When he opened the latch
the vapors uncurled and rose
and we leaned to watch
his arm disappear in Dry Ice.
(Mother had said *Don't touch, you'll stick.*)
We sat on the curb racing July

for the last, best licks
as creamy veins inched
down our arms, dripped on white socks.
Then night the felon hunched
over our street. Called
home, we whined and slouched.

It was years before I could tell
an oxymoron: the contradiction of Dry Ice;
before I dropped high-school
chemistry, bewildered by matter and valence.
          *solid carbon dioxide*
          *–78.5 degrees Centigrade*
Years before I touched your face.

# I WILL DRAW YOU THREE LINES

One leads to a country house in Finland,
with large windows opening onto a garden.
Everything's picked or fallen.
The man and woman who walk there
think they see a headstone beyond the pines
winter light wedges through.
They are trying to remember what they knew.
It is difficult to say at this distance
whether the man and woman have just taken
each other's hands, or are about to let go.

*

The second line leads to a field at high altitude
on which a team sport is being played.
The sky is at once falling
and rising from the grass, the stones,
engulfing the players in cold fire.
They hang in air, seem rather to dance.
Something is passed from one pair of outstretched
arms to the other. We cannot tell what.
Mountains used to enclose and define the players,
who now float in light from nowhere, everywhere.

*

Beginning at trees, the third line ends
in a landscape neither of us has seen.
Since I can only fill it with
what I know, it is made of lies.
Don't look away. There are no limbs to stumble on,
no instructions. Space, not emptiness.
Don't cross anything out yet.
If we reach this place together, let us call it
Hope, or Imagination, or Eyes,
and love each other for what we draw inside.

# III

## BETTER VISION

I'm not an unusual case.  Even my joke
about my arms not being long enough
to hold out the news is old stuff to Doc.
*Uncross your knees*, he says, and moves close
the iron mask.  The house lights go off
and on the far wall appear . . . letters, I suppose.
In another place I'd imagine
chromosomes or cells in mitosis.
Click click and before each eye the magician
produces, voilà, a *T*, an *F*, a diminutive *E*
and time hasn't entirely won
yet.  I am told not to blink away
the cobalt light aiming a direct hit
(the blue named for goblins in Germany);
next I am placed in the glare of an oncoming freight,
tied to the tracks but saved when the room
snaps heroically back so Doctor can note
the shape, color, and size of my visual jetsam.
Then, *Uncross your knees* again, and darkness,
nothing between us but a cone of light on the stem
he holds.  Every exam a woman has
by a man is gynecological.  I think of an onion-
eating eye man who exhaled and touched my face,
kissed me goodbye when I couldn't see at 14.
A dentist who gave the most painless, suave
injections and claimed to be nicer outside his office.
But today it's all eyes.  I'm either deranged or alive.
Or something between: the form in the chair, object
of his verb, patient, the one who must move
back to see.  Who sheds yellow tears in his Kleenex.

## FIRE POEM

I spend all morning building fires
to keep away thought, the brother of rain.

Meanwhile fire is set overnight on the leaves.
It rains for the sixth straight day.

My slicker grows downcast on the hook;
by the door, my boots wait for instructions.

I can't advise them.
I'm good for the worst of all reasons.

In the woods, red lizards dart from black rock
like tongues saying *wander*.

Henry at 83 dances, having burned back
his fields of wives, wars, cancers.

What recurs for a woman but rain
in the country of homefires and lovelight?

Twin devils grin from the andirons, propped
on forepaws, hind parts ablaze.

The stargazer says Capricorn
is the sign most given to depression.

Goat, scramble up
past the tree line, up where wind flames.

## HIS CALL

The phone rips me from a dream —
"Hello Sweetheart, I'm gonna feel your" —
and I'm awake enough to kill him.
I fall back on the pillow,

my heart crashing through the dark
while the Peter Lorre voice replays
until I want to wash my ear
want to shake you to be sure
after that voice like a searchlight.

The only light here is the clock face.
Suppose I were alone.
Suppose a fire escape,
a pay phone across the street
and someone leaning there, watching.

Is he a madman with other keys,
a businessman at nightly exercise, satisfied
that he can break dreams
and insert his own?

I creep downstairs, half expecting him.
Is he spreading jam on his toast?
Does he also wait behind glass
as the blue streets get safe?

# LADY'S WRITING DESK, CIRCA 1880

Matters of little consequence,
narrow, it says.
*Please come to tea*
*The embroidered pillowslips match*
*Dear James, Since you left for Princeton* . . .

The joiner was just taking orders,
we are often smaller. But
J. Austen at a lady's writing desk? M. Curie?

Relax, I tell myself.
Genius writes in the palm of its own hand,
writes on the world's lap, on the air.
Desks notwithstanding.

Still, something is ominous here.
This desk would thank any corner,
would never intrude
on the conversations of overstuffed chairs.
A hundred years later,
a child's business is too big to fit.

This desk made some man a fine wife.

## THE MAGIC RING

Oh I had a gold one
a signet ring I'd chew on
each night before sleep
unpeopled the country
under my bed.
*You could have swallowed it*
my father said
slipping it down on the awl
to take out the kinks,
make it fit for a pinky again.

But gold was nothing.
Gold was dull
beside what Post Cereals devised:
a glow-in-the-dark solar system
I could wear on my finger
for just 50¢ and 3 boxtops plus postage,
the planets shrunk to my size.

Summer was long that year.
In the mail it didn't come
and didn't, until I began
to believe my mother — *You can't*
*trust that baloney.*

Summer was long
in line at Astoria Pool
and on the fire escape,
waiting for rain.

The last Tuesday before school
the mailman delivered the box
so light it felt empty,
sealed with tape
my fingers shook to undo.

It was shiny black plastic,
too big for all but my tall man.
I ran to the closet
where we kept the dog
during thunderstorms,
where Mother kept the toilet plunger
and the Kotex

and there among the secrets
my own breath hot around me
stars took their places at my knuckle,
I ruled the stifling night.

# THE SPELLING-BEE AS FORESHADOWING

The auditorium swallowed
contenders alive
while the whole student body
was made to endure
Miss Riegel pronouncing the words
like life-terms.

We knew what was important:
arranging letters
like workclothes on a line.
*I* before *E* was order we could
count on. We knew
the maverick *weird*.

To be grade-school champ
I spelled *impeccable*,
a dashing stranger.
An angel bent to my ear
and whispered "Double *c*!"

In the citywide finals
I was tasting the win
when the judge gave me *fuchsia*.

Where was my angel
to warn of the snake,
the sly *s*?
What was the rule?

Later I looked up the word
and stared long
at that showy, pendant, crimson,
unspellable flower.

## PART I, PRIMARY EDUCATION
## IN THE PROVINCES

This basic: not
to jostle the air
to take as little
space as she can.

She sings from
the next room
crouched under a table.
When she burns
she uses their oxygen
so the large one
unfastens, uncages
his belt from its loops
until once the buckle . . .

They want her
as a portrait
contained
against the wall
small-mouthed
and stolid —
"Daughter of the Artist"
"Girl in the Shadows."
No one need
walk around her.

Later they wonder
why she longs
to be petite
starves herself
to become more lovable.
They scrimp
and send her
to a sunny place.

If to fade
is good
to vanish
must be excellent.
She gets A's.

Part II
will examine
How to Come Back.

# THE CHIROPRACTOR

Street-level, his office is the one
between the Center for the Esoteric Arts
and the door announcing LAWYER.
The receptionist in white prefixes
every comment to him with a "Doctor"
as if she can award degrees.

Inside the conference room he asks
you things he has no right to know
and marks the answers on a scoresheet.
Examining, he smiles to see
the iron hand-grip barely register
your strain, he stretches you

until you call him uncle,
then puts you on a table tilting
like a burial at sea. The largest man
who's ever stood above you says "Relax"
and grabs you. Something cracks . . .

you're in the alleys of an ancient dream
where when you tried to scream for help
no sound came out, you want to cry,
*you want to beat him up*
but you consented!

The chiropractor can adjust you until
he's Atlas. This pain needs movement —
off his table, on your feet and out the door
into the dear humidity of Boston
carrying the body's grief on your back.

# WOMEN NEAR SEA

*after a painting by Paul Delvaux*

Taking what's left of the sun
in high-necked, clinging dresses,

they look like each other
but do not recognize themselves.

They could be women of pleasure,
oddly prim as they wait by the houses.

Perhaps weather makes them sit so still
on parlor chairs outside the closed doors,

makes them not see or speak.
Perhaps they are wooden figures

all sprung on the hour, now stuck,
unable to get back inside the clocks.

The women's hands nest in their laps.
No salt wind bothers their hair,

their skirts long enough to hide everything.
Women could die in such heat in such dresses.

Behind a door someone is calling
*Martha* or *Mother* but she will not answer.

In the distance she swims with the others,
their fins parting the sea.

# THE LENGTH OF THE POOL

Relax! yells my teacher.
At the steamy window
branches obey snow.
I disobey her.

> Once, water was home
> no questions asked.
> Now this unknown
> distance beneath
> and its voice, Come
> with me, little girl . . .

I bob for breath,
each joint and muscle
straining to unflex.
Water takes resisters back.

> I accept the teacher's rule —
> body floats, I am proof —
> and the law she omits:
> mind's the sinker,
> the large-boned, the oaf.
> Mind learns the crawl.

Even if I cheat and backstroke
water doesn't shirk.
Overhead, new constellations.
I wheel, I levitate
past the 12-foot mark.

> Order's everything, as in birthdays
> or in making love.
> Evolution says first swim, then fly.
> And always move.

I lie down on the water
at what I hope's
the center of my life.
Fear is the dwarf
who makes me swim, count laps.

# A PLACE YOU OUGHT TO VISIT

The pain in my right side reminds me
there's a lot left to lose,
and not just appendices.

Pat Taylor had hers out in 5th grade
and showed the pink zipper.
She married Angelo,
who grew into a pusher

— but I'm far from my right side.
(Mind's little subterfuge.)

Still the body continues undiverted
from its treacheries.
While I swim, eat yogurt, climax

in the caves and tunnels
this or that takes aim,
plants a bomb.

Maybe this is It. Let guilt
soak those who didn't love me.

Flannery O'Connor, a pro,
said sickness is a place
you ought to visit
before the eighth wonder.

I look pain in the eye, try to
remember where else we've met.
When it folds hands and leans back,
it seems almost friendly.

Now I have made my way
through both sides,
passing myself in the middle —

a woman out in the rain,
between towns.

# THE DREAM CARRYING FURNITURE

### 1
I am lost between two cities,
reading your letter. You say you're down.
The alphabet breaks into runes as I read
but I keep the word *revere*.
When I reach *This means,*
the paper blows away.

### 2
I see the child crouched behind a rock.
Loudspeakers plead on his parents' behalf.
He darts out, jumps onto the tricycle,
pedals furiously, weaving a path
between grownups. When they recognize him
he leaps off and runs past me
turning and grinning, his eyes terrible and adult
in their dishes of shadow.

### 3
The man of hats kneels beside me
asking the impossible.
His voice blooms in my ear,
the room is a garden I feed with my breath.
Slowly his fingertips polish my arm
until he can see his face there.

### 4
I stand behind the curtain
while the accountant calls from the driveway.
Someone has carried my couch onto the lawn.
Curled on it, a woman,
my child, reads "The Wind in the Door."
I have no place to sit.

### 5
Someone speaks this in my dream:
*We fall, with clumsy grace, through our lives.*

LIFE IN THE SOIL

Diorama, American Museum of Natural History,
New York City


The display says *Life in the soil*
*is ordinarily invisible*
*but it is an important factor*
*in the existence of*
*life above.*


In floor-to-ceiling showcases, the seasons last.
Around me in the dark hall,
kids carrying notebooks yell
that they've found the answers.


I am facing Winter.
The farmer with earmuffs sinks
to his knees in snow, appears to give thanks
for these horses, this grain, the woodstove
in his kitchen.  He is the sieve
seasons flow through, while in the soundproof
room, the dark two-thirds of the case, life


happens in the soil.  Beetle larvae wait
and the earthworm ties himself in a square knot
finding his answers.
The white-footed mouse, squatter
in the mole's tight sleeve, chews on bulbs,
the chipmunk blows a bubble,
fills it with acorns and leaves, wriggles
in.  The toads hunch in their camouflage jackets.
They are all important factors.


In fourth grade Miss Benton's class
came here.  Behind the mummies,
Gregory Martin touched me.
I cross-section time
and he's here in this room.

So is my favorite aunt, Viola, who today
is moved back to the hospital
bleeding from a place ordinarily invisible.

Up from the soil of memory
comes the Viola who
led me underground
at Federal Reserve where she typed and filed
in the basement, near gold.
Who developed a rash in the sun,
the red pre-cancers I carry on
itching and stinging in the August night,
awake till the last train goes by with its freight.

In darkness life takes hold,
we others the earth for blond boys
and favorite aunts. In us they build.
Viola, what you were *is*.
Here in the exhibit called Spring
the farmer drinks at his well.
Next to tulips, stones crown through the soil.

IV

# A COLLAGE: THE NATIONAL STANDARD

as set in *The Elementary Spellingbook*
by Noah Webster, 1880

The good boy will not tear his book.
A girl can toast a piece of bread.
The devil is the great adversary of man.
There is a near intimacy between
drunkenness, poverty, and ruin.

Pure water and good air are salutary.
The dysentery is a painful disease.
Little girls and boys love to ride in a wagon.
Few men can afford to keep a coach.
To filch is to steal. We must not filch.

I can play when my task is done.
The sun will set at the close of the day.
The eye is a very tender organ, and one
of the most useful members of the body.

Doors are hung on hinges.
Chilblains are sores caused by cold.
Shut the gate and keep the hogs out of the yard.
To purloin is to steal.

To frounce is to curl or frizzle, as the hair.
The ladies adorn their heads with tresses.
Humility is the prime ornament of a Christian.
You must be good, or you cannot be happy.

The first joint of a man's thumb is one inch long.
Six boys can sit at one long bench.
It is useful to keep very exact accounts.
Larceny is theft, and liable to be punished.

I have seen the full moon.
Friday is just as lucky a day as any other.
I wish I had a bunch of sweet grapes.
Dig up the weeds and let the corn grow.
The wind will drive the dust in our eyes.

[53]

## VETERANS DAY, 1981

In last week's *New York Times* I read
the First Lady's announcement from the White
House: a joke writer was hired until it all blew
over, the enemy's cheap shots
about expensive gowns and china.  Appease
your critics with a laugh, she said.  Disarm

them.  Meanwhile the paper's full of arms
deals.  "Capability" is spread
worldwide like a synonym for peace
and nobody needs to see the whites
of anyone's eyes to fire the shot
heard round the big blue

marble that nobody's left to hear.  This blue-
print for disaster went to charm
school.  It wouldn't *really* shoot
us out of history, out of the red.
It'd just be a kind of joke to write
till the pressure was off.  We'd aim to please.

I remember how my father eased
his grief when FDR died.  He blew
three loud blasts into his white
handkerchief, covered his face with his arm
and looked up much later, redder
than sunburn.  The shot-

glass came down from the closet, and he shot
loss dead.  I was too young to be pleased
he cared so much.  I only saw that grown man red.
Now I find myself singing the blues
for what I think we've lost and will.  I'm alarmed:
when did I last love my leader?  White-

washes aside, who wears a white
hat for us?  Maybe those who make moonshots,

not arms. I want arms —
*these things attached to our shoulders* — in their place.
Starting with language, the true blue
chip. Orwell knew. They're worse if we call them "reds."

Bloodshot eyes mean I drink too much red wine while the blue sky
darkens. Think of the world silent as a white page where, once,
someone with an arm, a hand, could have written *Stop. Please.*

# HANDEDNESS, A RIGHT-HANDED VIEW

As right grips the pen, follows orders,
covers the pages with meaning,
grinning crookedly left marches off
behind the mirror to unmake the message.

The hands dress for their parts:
right in carpenter's jeans, each pocket
stuffed with utility; in surgical gown,
in tweeds, in athletic support.
Left in an opera cape, keys underneath.
In pointed-toe shoes with taps on the heels,
in darkglasses and Stetson.

Right guides the spoon, left spills the milk.
Right plays melody, left deep contrapunto.
Right is every good boy, deserves fun.
Left is truant and may not graduate.

While right holds the flashlight
left presses the circle, showing his bones.
While right pushes-up at the "Y"
left limps away from the streetlamp.
While right smoothes the sheets
left twitches under the pillow.

Right bounces the sun up and down
over the edge of day.
Left hides in the trees until nightfall.
Then he calls from the branches,
a cry heard through the windows in dreams,
*This way. Follow me.*

# IN NASHVILLE

The aging country music star makes his comeback
every night at nine. His jokes are ethnic
and he kisses nervous housewives on the cheek

between numbers. They blush like virgins.
Just to show how upright this fun
is, he brings a real one —

Daddy's little girl — into the act. He flirts
and bends his face for her to kiss. What
could be more innocent than that?

While he sings his countless tears,
he counts on theirs.
Couples dance too close for strangers.

If his songs are true they'll leave this place
together, be good, get another chance.
The married ones won't divorce.

At tables outside the spotlight, folks look on
in pairs, in groups, and all alone.
The hostess serves another round of bourbon.

Someone wonders how the darkened room
appears by day. Someone tilts toward home.
Travelers feel this is the town they come from,

forget who waits with radio turned low.
They tell secrets they won't know tomorrow
when they wake, tongues dry and raw.

# THE VILLAGE CYCLIST

Every day and weather, he's our shadow.
On the squat cycle with highrise handlebars
— the kind our kids scorned years ago —
dressed grownup in a mustache, he's here:
a circus act riding round and round
the neighborhood, patterning his time.

The audience doesn't need to mind
or solve him. He's no problem.
When dogs pursue him, when teenagers throw
curses, he waves, and rings the bell.

Sometimes he rides as if he's chauffeur
of a limousine, sometimes tourist: all
eyes left and right, never saw
a house before. Or he races, neck
thrust forward, chinning the front wheel,
he rides to get a lost thing back.

On a bicycle that size he has to pedal double
to reach the local liquor store,
Post Office, Convenient Market. Then finds
he can't remember why he came.
His mother forgets too. Are they kinder,
lacking our subtlety to cause each other pain?

We hope that nature compensates somehow;
bats are saved by sonar.
I think he could be taught — by *me*
perhaps, I could hire him to wash the car.
You say it's good he rides, what would he do
with so much energy. We're almost sure

he's happy when he stands and coasts,
clasped against the air.

# POEM FOUND IN AN ENSIGN'S JOURNAL

aboard the submarine *Lionfish*, 1942

A man must contract to fit
through these passageways.
I tell you there must be nothing
left of him but nerve.

Nothing soft here or breakable
but the windows on gauges,
the two glass eyes on their stalks.
Over the stainless sinks our own eyes
look back at us in steel.

Our luxuries are: coffee 24 hours a day,
more pay, and the girls
who smile over our bunks, who live
where the sun reaches.
Whatever else blooms here is red,
a garden of valves and alarms.

This half-fish, half-fire
sings through the dark
as we solo in dreams.
Last night Forbes yelled
*the Momsen's gone*
and I couldn't drop off again.

If sleep shuts like a 300-lb. door
in the mind's chambers
I still hear the alert, see the child
running toward me stumble
and sink in the high grass

---

Momsen: an artificial lung used for escaping in depths of up to
100 feet.

or I watch silver milkweed
coast down the afternoon
beetles shine in the dirt.
I climb trees, I eat plums.

When we come home — and by God we will —
there will be no talk of this.
I will lie in the back field
smelling mown hay, with summer
on my face, and my life
caked on my lips like salt.

# THE INVALID

I lie still, in the middle of the country.
A flock of woolly birds flies over the quilt
pocking the gingham, flies over
my dumb legs and off the edge of the bed.

If I could, I would follow them and go further,
out of this room where light falters
on floorboards, makes stiff progress
over the wide afternoons of my life,

I would follow beyond the voice of the saw
speaking its sentence under my window —
John cutting posts to fence the east pasture —
beyond him field and horses
and the last grove of cedar, to the border
of that ocean I have never seen, I would cross.

The slow pendulum of the clock in the hall
knocks like a cane on my door.
Nothing will happen till lunch.
I will read *The Clarion* until sleep asserts itself
like a husband claiming his rights,
and I yield to those thighs.

Sometimes, draped with covers, I cannot see
where bed stops and I begin.  I grow flat
and soft, they air me and change me.
I hold the ceiling in place with my eyes.
I call the names of my bed: *bedtime, bedsore,
bedpan, bedrock, bedlam*, and sometimes I wish

for madness, the mind hobbled in its cell
while the body careens into summer,
into the grand-right-and-left of wheat,
the sinuous notes of the lark.  All the world
is a thing in motion!  What am I, what world am I in?

Last night I saw, like Ezekiel,
*the spirit of the living creature*
*was in the wheels.*  Four great wheels
hurtled toward me out of the broken sky,
I tried to run but my bones stuck in amber,
I could not I could not.
My cry rocked the pillow, woke John.
For comfort, he said we never die in dreams.

Whatever I want now must come to me.
I am the vortex that sucks itself in,
I am the child, the closest to ground.
My eyes enlarge with their power
to see life in its smallest dimensions:
spiders and dust motes and shadows.
The drummer at each of my wrists.

## STELLA'S DUMP

Francestown, New Hampshire, 1980

Begin at the top, then, with the rusted rake
sticking out of the ferrous heap like some
buried king's sceptre; from there make
your eye travel down the staggering sum
of disjointed parts, a compost of artifacts.
Breathe deeply the smell of decay. The treasure
of ruins surrounds you, leans in, these wrecks
profusely adopted, then left in the weather.
Wherever you look, another peak in the range
around the crumbling house, another cache
tucked into folds of the woods, that great sponge.
Now the door opens, the owners approach.
She says you're lucky. They were leaving for the day.
He says, "You never can tell what I'm goin' to do."

*

A trailer piled full past the windows,
cycle frames, a fence, some plastic pools,
a legless piano, mufflers, fenders, saws,
a tractor, corrugated pipes, hand-drills,
umbrellas, chains, a trumpet bell, transmissions,
box cameras, tires, coalstoves, steering wheels,
truck beds and cabs, steel cables, washing machines,
windshield wipers, screendoors, sinks, and bottles,
*7-Up, You Like It, It Likes You.*
Enough, please, you want it to stop, right?
but you're inside already, caught now
and maybe they too wanted to call a halt,
the mother and father of junk, but something undid
them, something they'd lost once, or never had.

*

He gums a plug of tobacco; grinning, spits
between you, wants to buy a car today.
You scan the woods, from here count six
that squat, relieved among the trees.
One's packed with dogfood, rope, and hats.
The rooster crows. The woman brings her hand-
made gloves to sell, explains her teeth are out,
it's early. Think of the two of them in bed
inside the house that replicates this yard,
the stuff impelling them to lie more close
where moon hacks out a path across the boards.
Even toothless, desire stalks this place.
Think of him stepping from trousers stiff with dirt,
of her unwinding the wiry hair from its knot.

*

This is hardest, the green Chevy Impala
angled uphill into four birches,
wipers arrested mid-sweep, vertical,
as if they've given up trying to work
the pine needles off. Meanwhile rust
pits the roof, metastasizes down.
The gauges, clock, and ashtray don't exist.
Beneath a net of cobwebs the seat is strewn
with letters to Mr. Maurice Beck: most
from Memorial Hospital, one from Neshoba Valley
Radiological Associates, a bill for three sets
of carotid arteriograms, June '72.
His pension envelopes to Eva Beck.
Sometimes you wish to Christ you didn't look.

*

But since you did — trespassed here — and found
a story junked in these New Hampshire woods,
retrieve them now, Maurice and Eva. Where wind
is sifting leaves, sun ramming clouds,
stand them near trees and let them drink

the rain from fallen headlight sockets, chase
the cat asleep on their Impala's trunk,
and hear the woman talking to her geese
and eat the kernels scattered in the mud.
Put them in the backseat, have them touch
the way they did before the doctors said
it. For you their story is contagious, the itch
a mangy dog attacks with canines bared.
You visit this time, chew until it bleeds.

# EATING OCTOBER

In this yellow
down-dropping of aspen
I want to open
my mouth the way
a child tongues
the first flakes
I want to take
it all, binge

lick the crystal jackets
from the grass
and let its color rise
get its breath back

swallow the lines
sun draws between limbs,
the tightropes for worms
those champions

and bring
indoors the paper ghost-
town, taste
nasturtiums and wings

## TRICKS DURING A STORM

The jay, that airforce general of the yard,
plumps himself like a pillow, having landed hard
on winter branches, shakes the hand of tree.
He tries to lose the weight of water falling resolutely
down all morning long. Meanwhile his squadron hides
in evergreens. He takes command, yells Up, and flies.

*

The thin man under lights, Prince Legerdemain,
throws back his cape, announces he'll explain.
Meaning: observe, here comes the scarf trick.
Crimson, canary, indigo — all gauzy at his neck,
admitting air and smoke. The women in the audience
are rapt. He wears such scarves unto his last appearance.

*

She is the house divided, standing anyway. Looks plumb
though leaning toward an absent name
she's spoken, immoderately affirmative
for all that flames and sinks (like certain loves)
and darkens dark. To ratify the world with other names than
bird, rain, house, when it knocks she says Come in.

*

This one has craft who turns back waters when they seep
through foundations as a man and woman sleep
together not entirely. Where frozen ground
abuts concrete, the man awake now piles the mound
of gravel, banks the walls with something hard,
unsentimental. He takes command, makes good. And it is good.

# POEM IN SEARCH OF DIFFERENT ENDINGS

This autumn, squirrels litter the road
on their backs, their sides,
in every posture of dead.
Surplus acorns, the experts nod,
lure them from the woods
by batallions. The red
jells where they couldn't hide.

And while we're eating lunch this mild
October day, the radio news is bad.
A 727 down, 100 souls aboard.
We keep chewing as if we haven't heard.
The principle is entropy: hazard,
the sharp turns that pervade
the system, the sudden Great Divide.

The bumper of the Pontiac ahead
says "Prayer changes things." I'd
say *Work*, and work to find another word
than loss — one to parade
through the streets, to break like bread.
But the habits of my head
raise up a boy, newly slid

away at 17. There's no excuse for God!
And furthermore I'm sick of being sad
this fall, of beasts too ragged
to find the beauty under, of carrion birds.
Bring on a serenade!
The world, that symphony of mud,
sings at me loudly, *World*.

V

STUDYING SKY

1
A man used to stare
at a green hospital ceiling
and wish, just once,
to sleep under a skylight.

One summer night the pumps yielded
to the roil in his chest.
Starring, held in the ring of light,
he was too far ahead to hear anyone.
Down the hall a radio played Chopin,
the popular version called, in the 40's,
"Till the End of Time."

Someone rested her hand, lightly she thought,
on his. But when she lifted it, her fingers
stayed: he was less himself than who touched him.

Outside, cobalt spilled down the air
    *cobalt, that word from a Crayola box*
    *Henny-Penny, the sky is falling . . .*
She who was there from the start said
Now he has the whole sky.

2
Deaf in my hermetic, 6th-floor office
I have a view of Logan Airport,
the sky and ocean in suspension,
the harbor spread before me like a lap.

I can't see the woman riding Amtrak
or the Eastern Shuttle that takes
her husband among suitcases and mailbags.

A 747 heads toward me until
I think I see the pilot's face;
then it slips into the haze, is gone.
My father belongs to the sky.

[71]

3

And I felt your life empty into mine
the way I pour the last drops
of milk into a fuller container,

I saw our two shadows overlap on the wall
and my heart knocked, stammered —

I felt you work, hover; I waited
for you to deliver your life
with a shrug, a set of the jaw

as if it were a small
thing you'd determined to do,

as if you'd surfaced from your dream.

4

    the thin-lipped man in a Stetson
    with the brim drawn over his eyes
    passes through the crowd
    on the subway platform

    something shines at his side
    something cold used in the woods

    he's out of reach
    raising the axe
    over the head of my son

I wake, and he's rescued.
*Rescue, subway, dream* — all opposites of *sky.*

5

Father unwith me
name that I say that no one can answer
one who is out of the school of the world

if you'd asked
I'd have found you a gun,
I was that kind of pacifist.

How often you wished
and I thought
*Let him sky!*

still you turned,
asked for news
of the world you were leaving.

So I came to know nothing
and gave my ignorance a home
and called it not *heavens*, but *sky*.

No one stands between me
and sky
but the mutinous air,
the fallible roof of my house.

# QUARRY

*At this stage we are not concerned with whether beds are overturned. This point will be discussed later.*
    *— New Hampshire Geological Bulletin, No. 4*

You joke about axe murders when we find
a pair of jean shorts on the ground.
But danger isn't in these woods,
it's on the path between us.

My shoes are wrong — no traction —
and the bulletin goes vague on distance.
Two high school boys direct us,
"Fork off left."

I want to find some father here.
I think he is my prey, the man
so intimate with stone
its dust has settled in his lungs.

Meanwhile we cast us in a Hitchcock thriller,
can't decide quite what will be the crime.

*This quarry lies in the heart of the intensely deformed
Appalachian tectonic belt.*

Foundation walls and pits have left
the buildings' footprints.
Lintels carved *1884*, *Hope*, *Charity* lie
supporting nothing in the leaves,
and *Faith* is gone.

The quarry rises like a mist
but close we see how solidly it waits.
On a rock someone has sprayed the sign
for peace, as if the place
were not enough.

We lean uphill between the trees
and water, not falling into each.
If I fall into you, you say,
you will not save me.

I try to put the carver here,
to fill the woods with blasting,
pry the granite loose, send mica
glinting down the air,

to excavate the core.

*This rock is considered to be Middle Devonian, characterized*
*by the appearance of forests and amphibians between 405*
*and 345 million years ago.*

Thought stumbles, panting at the ledge.
A bluejay snips remaining daylight
into scraps almost too small to use.
Let the trees moan, the water sound
more deep than we can tell, the bright
backs of leaves float the possible. Now.
The only time in which we grow.

> Salamanders, wary of air, thrash in silt
> in the shelter of clouds passing over
> they wait
>
> smooth-skinned
> for change, try holding them and they
> jump from the burning hotel of your hand

My father hangs between air and water,
breathing through a plastic tube

and we too hover,
lustrous, rich in impurities.

*As the time of maximum stress passed, the temperature*
*dropped. This was accompanied by further*
*shearing and slippage of rocks.*


On Marriage:

We live in an age of lost arts.
No one can do my father's work
and when an old metronome breaks
no one can fix it.
I look for the human hand
reaching from stone,
wood, cloth — humanity's grasp
on the world — and see machines
behind machines. We live
in an age of great comforts
but small satisfaction.
Our telephone-answering tapes
talk while we shut ourselves off,
lose the art of living together.
To marry once is to be a troglodyte.
We live in a time of replacement,
not repair. To marry once
is to settle, to compromise.
What the language held "a mutual
pledge" means "to give up."
This is the age of the self:
self-image, self-realization,
self-defense. And surely love begins
in the walled city of self
but not to set up house and never leave,
the earth in a new Ptolemaic system.
George Eliot says in a poem
*Life is justified by love*
— is proved right, pardoned.
I have lived and been married to you so
long I grow moral. Listen,
I forgive you. Forgive me.

On Running:

Some things are too broken.
Leave them behind, sprint
till nothing counts.  O pow-

erful disturbance, you
waving at me, you in
your famous blue shorts,

when you come running by I want to leap
up from my desk and tear out, coatless, fling
myself across the road, an obstacle
too great for you to vault or circumvent,
a presence to be dealt with, searched.

Instead I let you pass. The road falls down,
I stand to glimpse your head between the trees.
Practicing, I let you disappear.


*The errors produced by the items listed above would be
presumably compensatory.*


        *   *   *

I hold to adamantine facts.
Mason's *Bicentennial History,* leatherbound,
says Alexander McDonald of Cambridge
bought the quarry in 1867.
At its peak, employed two hundred workmen,
two blacksmiths, and a boy to shuttle tools.
Steam powered the machines that polished
what the earth gave rude.

We don't have far but we have deep
so call me all the names
that we can lend each other.
No wonder we can't sleep.
Between our houses, flames
along the wire alarm our

little rest.  No time or use
for dreaming, even.  Stars tack
the sky's black map, moon rises,
spreads a sheet of light across
the field where aspen quake,
contemplate a pair who have to lose . . .

Receding, you make me disappear.

John B. Hill wrote, 1872

> If this state of things becomes permanent . . .
> material is inexhaustible
> and the railroad facilities abundant . . .
> this place must meet with a prosperous advance.

*Permanent, inexhaustible, abundant, advance*:
words that don't belong to us
who see the world run out,
abetted by ourselves.
We read the crumbled lintels,
count the empty cellar-holes.
The entire village — houses, railroad station,
company store, post office — repossessed by woods.

McDonald Quarry sent granite to New York's
State Capitol, to the Metropolitan
Museum of Art.  One monument cut here
rode to California in five freight cars, prone.

Sic transit gloria mundi, sic transit stone and carvers,
lovers: the tall lie down.

*The rocks of the quadrangle are obviously the result of
a major orogenic episode.*

From a mountain top, we see the way
the earth has folded into rhythmic

scalloped ranges, how hidden
pressures contoured every face.
We see to Boston.
Rock music's blaring from a car
parked at the overlook,
two kids are smoking pot.
Light fingers through the clouds
to choose those trees, that farm.
We see so far the view becomes
an analogue for future.
A yellow arrow painted on a rock
points east and west at once.

*These events brought the deformational and intrusive history
of the quadrangle to a close, and erosion, interrupted only
by glaciation, has ensued to this day.*

I came to excavate the core.

You ask me how I want to say goodbye.
Quick, no waver
at the threshold or behind the wheel
and dry as stone.

I am the hunted and the hunter
and the hound who's thrown
the entrails for a prize.
Intruder everywhere! this loudest heartbeat,
mine.

# ACKNOWLEDGMENTS

Some of the poems which appear here have been published in the following magazines and are reprinted with permission:

ASPECT, No. 76, "Poem Found in an Ensign's Journal"

HOLLOW SPRING REVIEW OF POETRY, "A Place You Ought to Visit"

NIMROD, "Women Near Sea"

PLOUGHSHARES, "Stonecarver," "Stonecarver's Wife," "Veterans Day, 1981"

POETRY, "A Collage: The National Standard" (1980), "In Nashville" (1980), "I Will Draw You Three Lines" (1980), "Better Vision" (1981), "Like Musical Chairs" (1981); these poems © in year listed by The Modern Poetry Association

POETRY NORTHWEST, "Now, While We Have the Body Before Us," "The Dream Carrying Furniture"

POETRY Now, "Eating October," "The Magic Ring"

PRAIRIE SCHOONER, "Domestica" (1978), "Conditional" (1980), "Handedness, A Right-Handed View" (1980), "Life in the Soil" (1980), "Poem in Search of Different Endings" (1980), "Stonecarver, Restoring" (1980), "Driving to Worcester in Snow" (1982), "Lady's Writing Desk, Circa 1880" (1982), "Quarry" (1982), "Spring" (1982), "Studying Sky" (1982), "The Cardinal Causes Me to Say *Oh*" (1982); these poems © in year listed by the University of Nebraska Press

TENDRIL, "Reading Father," "Stella's Dump," "What Shall We Name the Snow?"

THE AGNI REVIEW, "Shore-Walking"

THE BOSTON MONTHLY, "Fire Poem"

THE REAL PAPER, "The Spelling-Bee as Foreshadowing"

THE SEATTLE REVIEW, "The Invalid," Vol. IV, No. 1

THE VIRGINIA QUARTERLY REVIEW, "Dry Ice"

Lines from "Men Loved Wholly Beyond Wisdom," from *The Blue Estuaries* by Louise Bogan, © 1923, 1929, 1930, 1931, 1933, 1934, 1935, 1936, 1937, 1938, 1941, 1949, 1951, 1952, 1954, 1957, 1958, 1962, 1963, 1964, 1965, 1966, 1967, 1968 by John McPhee; reprinted by permission of Farrar, Straus & Giroux, Inc.

A section of "Back, Says the Voice" appeared in *The Loneliness Factor* by Carole Oles, © 1979 by Texas Tech University.